THIS BOOK BELONGS TO

This edition published by HarperCollins Publishers Ltd 1996
First published 1959 by Sampson Lowe
© Darrell Waters Limited 1958 as to all text and illustrations
Enid Blyton's signature mark and the word 'NODDY' are Registered
Trade Marks of Enid Blyton Ltd
ISBN 0 00 198247-8
Printed and bound in Italy

NODDY GOES TO SEA

BY *Enid Blyton*

CONTENTS

Collins

A Division of HarperCollins*Publishers*

NODDY RUSHED OFF TO THE BIG SHIP, AND THERE
WAS TUBBY STANDING ON THE DECK

6

1. NODDY'S WASHING DAY

"IT'S Monday morning—washing day!" said Noddy, and he looked out of the window. "Good—it's a fine, sunny, windy morning—just right for washing!"

He got his little washing-tub ready, and fetched his dirty clothes. Then how busy he was! The lather rose up in the tub almost to Noddy's hot face, and bubbles flew in the air.

"See me rub,
See me scrub
In my little washing-tub,"

sang Noddy, rubbing hard at his dirty little vest.

"Hear me sing
While I wring
Vests and socks and everything!"

7

And there was Noddy wringing out the soap and water, singing at the top of his voice all the time.

"Now you'll go
For a blow,
Flapping in a happy row!"

shouted Noddy, and rushed out to hang the wet clothes on the line. Mrs Tubby Bear was hanging her washing out, too, and she laughed at little Noddy as he ran out, carrying his basket of clean washing.

"I never knew such a little fellow for singing about everything," said Mrs Tubby. "Never! It's really very nice to live next door to you, Noddy."

"Oh — I didn't know you were listening," said Noddy. "Where's little Tubby Bear today, Mrs Tubby? Would he like to come out in the car with me and help me do my shopping?"

"He's in bed," said Mrs Tubby. "He's been naughty again. He was very rude to me and wouldn't even carry out my washing-basket for me! I really don't know what's the matter with him these days. I've sent him to bed for an hour."

"Oh dear," said Noddy, his head nodding very fast. "You should have asked me—I'd have carried that washing-basket for you! Isn't it a lovely morning, Mrs Tubby—our washing will soon be nice and dry! And away he went indoors, singing loudly again.

"See it blow
In a row,
Flipping-flapping to and fro!"

Mrs Tubby went into her house smiling. Noddy made himself a cup of cocoa, and then decided he had better go and clean the car. "Washing day for you too, car," he said, as he went to open his garage door.

Noddy had a look at his washing as he went by. Ah — it was already getting nice and dry! He disappeared into the garage, and was soon busy there.

He heard Mrs Tubby Bear's front gate click and saw her going off to do her shopping. Then,

after a minute, he heard something else. What was it?

"It sounds like water splashing about," said Noddy to himself, and he peeped out to see. Good gracious! It was little Tubby Bear in the next garden, with the hose—but he wasn't watering the flowers.

"Goodness—he's watering Mrs Tubby's nice dry

washing and making it all wet again!" said Noddy, in amazement, and he ran to the wall at once. "Tubby! What do you think you're doing? Stop that at once! That's your mother's washing you're watering."

"I know. I'm doing it on purpose," said Tubby. "She was horrid to me this morning. She sent me to bed! Now she wants me to water the flowers!"

"Well, stop watering her WASHING!" yelled Noddy.

"Shan't," said Tubby. "Well—yes, I will then—I'll water yours instead!"

And he pointed the hose over the wall and, splishy-splash, the water drenched poor Noddy's nice dry washing. Then Tubby pointed the hose at Noddy and watered *him!*

"You must be mad," said Noddy, feeling the water trickling down his neck. "What's the matter with you lately, Tubby? STOP, you're soaking me!"

"I can't," said Tubby, beginning to giggle. "I c-c-can't stop. You look so funny!"

"All right—two can play at that game," said

11

Noddy, angrily, and he ran to get his own hose and turn on the tap. SPLOSH! A great jet of water splashed all over Tubby Bear, and he fell down in surprise.

"AND WHAT IS ALL THIS?" said a loud voice suddenly, and, dear me, it was Mr Plod the policeman, who had come up very quietly indeed. He was MOST astonished to see all this watering going on.

"Oh! Oh, Mr Plod—it was Noddy who started it all," said Tubby. "He—he was very naughty—he took his hose and watered all my mother's nice dry washing. Just look at it!"

"Ooooooh, you bad, untruthful bear!" shouted Noddy, swinging round, quite forgetting he still had his hose in his hand. "Oh, sorry, Mr Plod! I didn't MEAN to water

MR PLOD WAS *MOST* ASTONISHED TO SEE ALL THIS
WATERING GOING ON

you, really I didn't. Oh my goodness, now *I'm* in trouble too—and all because of that mean, untruthful Tubby Bear. I won't stay here another minute."

And Noddy turned off the tap, leapt into his car and drove off at top speed out of the gate, still dripping with water. Oh dear, oh dear—what a thing to happen on a nice windy washing morning!

2. BAD LITTLE TUBBY BEAR!

NODDY needn't have rushed off in such a hurry. Somebody had seen all that happened! It was Miss Fluffy Cat, who had been passing by on the other side of the road. She ran across to poor, wet Mr Plod and dried him with her hanky.

"Don't blame little Noddy," she said. "It really wasn't his fault! Tubby has been a bad little bear for a long time—and when his mother went out shopping this morning he came out and hosed her nice dry washing—and Noddy tried to stop him."

"Ah—I see—and Tubby watered Noddy's washing too, I suppose," said Mr Plod, shaking the water off his helmet. "And then watered Noddy, and . . ."

"Yes—and so Noddy got *his* hose, and I don't blame him," said Miss Fluffy Cat, swinging her tail in quite a rage. "That Tubby! He rode his scooter *right* into me yesterday, and didn't even say he was sorry."

"I shall speak to your parents tonight, Tubby," said Mr Plod, sternly. "Just as soon as your father gets home."

"Everybody's horrid to me," wailed Tubby. "I shall run away. Yes, I shall! I shall run away to sea! Nobody wants me. Nobody loves me. Boo-hoo-hoo!"

And he ran indoors, not even bothering to turn off the tap.

"Waste of good water!" said Mr Plod crossly, turning it off himself. "Just you wait till this evening, young Tubby!"

"I'll run away!" yelled Tubby, putting his head out of his bedroom

16

window. "Then you'll all be sorry!"

Well, that night when Noddy got home, tired after a long day of driving people to the station, and to the market, and goodness knows where else, he heard all that had happened. Mrs Tubby Bear told him, dabbing her eyes with a hanky.

"Mr Plod came and complained. And Mr Tubby Bear was furious with Tubby, and Tubby was very rude again and wouldn't say he was sorry. All he said was that he was going to run away and never come back, because nobody loved him!"

"He won't run away," said Noddy, hugging Mrs Tubby. "Don't you worry! He'll soon be his nice self again. He's just being silly."

17

But goodness me, in the middle of the night young Tubby Bear *did* run away! Yes—a small figure crept out of the back door and ran quietly down the road with a little bag and disappeared into the dark night. Master Tubby was gone!

Noddy didn't know anything about it till Mr and Mrs Tubby Bear came knocking at his door early in the morning. "Come in!" called Noddy.

And in they came, Mrs Tubby crying, and Mr Tubby holding a note in his hand.

"Tubby's gone," he said. "Look at this."

Noddy took the note and read it. This is what it said:

Nobody Loves me so I've run away to sea. Tubby

"Oh *dear!*" cried Noddy. "Has he really gone?"

"Yes. That's why we've come to you," said Mr Tubby Bear. "He's taken a little bag of things with him. We think he's gone down to the river, to the jetty there, where steamers and ships tie up. Some of them sail out to sea, you know. Oh, Noddy — could you get out your car, and go off to the river, and see if you can stop him?"

"Oh yes — yes, of course I will," said Noddy at once. "I'm almost dressed. I'll get my car. Oh goodness, what a thing to happen! Don't cry, Mrs Tubby. I'll bring him back, you'll see!"

And Noddy got out his car, waved goodbye, and

19

set off at top speed, hoping that Mr Plod wouldn't see him racing by. He had to stop at the garage to get some petrol — and who should come trotting up, looking as bouncy as ever, but the Bumpy-Dog! Noddy didn't see him till Bumpy had leapt lovingly up and knocked him over.

"Oh, BUMPY! You've made me sit in a puddle! Don't lick me like that. Get *off* me, Bumpy. I'm in a hurry, do you hear? Oh, hallo, Tessie Bear! Pull Bumpy off me, will you? I'm in a dreadful hurry. Tubby Bear has run away to sea, and I'm off to stop him. Bumpy, go AWAY!"

"Oh dear! What made Tubby do such a silly thing?" asked Tessie. But Noddy really couldn't stop. He pushed Bumpy away, jumped into his car, and drove off, waving.

BUMPY LEAPT UP LOVINGLY AND KNOCKED
NODDY INTO A PUDDLE!

21

"WUFF!" Bumpy ran after the car and leapt in too, his tail thumping against Noddy in delight. He began to lick Noddy's left ear lovingly.

"I've washed that ear already this morning," said Noddy, pushing him away. "Bumpy, get out, please! PLEASE, Bumpy."

But Bumpy sat himself down firmly. He loved Noddy very much, and he wasn't going to miss this ride for anything. What a dog!

Noddy sighed and carried on, driving fast. WHAT a pity Bumpy had to choose to come with him just now!

3. ALL VERY SURPRISING

NODDY drove on till he came to the river. His car ran on to the big stone jetty, where one steamer and several ships were safely tied to mooring posts. Was there any sign of Tubby?

Noddy left his car on the jetty and went to look for him. "Stay in the car," he said to Bumpy. "And look after it for me. See if you can make yourself useful for once."

Noddy went to the nearest ship, and hailed a sailor doll on board. "Hey! Have you seen a little brown bear anywhere?"

"One went on board that big sailing ship at the end there!" said the sailor, pointing. "You'd better hurry if you want him—the ship's just casting off."

Noddy rushed off to the big ship. Yes — the ropes were being cast off — and there was

Tubby Bear standing on the deck, looking rather lonely!

"Tubby! Come back!" yelled Noddy, but Tubby shook his head.

"I'll come and get you!" shouted Noddy, and climbed on board the ship. And just at that very moment the last rope was cast off, and the ship floated away from the stone jetty!

"Oh, no!" said Noddy, in alarm. "Oh, turn back the ship! Look, I've left my car there!"

Bumpy-Dog was most upset to see Noddy jump on board the ship. He leapt out of the car and raced down the jetty—and oh dear, the car ran down too. Bumpy leapt into the water to swim to Noddy and the car fell over the jetty-side, and went into the river with a most tremendous SPLASH!

"My CAR! My car's fallen in!" yelled Noddy, dancing in alarm. "Stop the ship! Pick up my car. It will sink! Listen to it hooting for help!"

"Parp-parp!" said the car, bobbing about on the water. "PARPARP-PARPARPARP!" It was mostly made of wood so it didn't sink, but it certainly sounded very upset.

Two sailors ran to the side when they heard the loud hooting. "A car!" said one. "Does it belong to you, little fellow? And is that a dog swimming to it?"

"Yes, oh yes!" said Noddy. "That's the Bumpy-Dog. He was supposed to be looking after the car. Goodness, he's getting into it — whatever does he think he can do?"

"Better fling a rope and lasso the car," said the sailor. "Then we can tow it behind us. What

25

about the dog? Here, tie a rope to this lump of wood—if he's got any sense he'll jump on it and we can drag him in."

"What the Captain's going to say to all this I *don't* know," said the second sailor.

Soon the lump of wood was flung into the water, and Noddy yelled to Bumpy-Dog. "Get on it, Bumpy! Bumpy, do you hear me? Get out of the car, you'll sink it! We'll pull you up if you get on the piece of wood."

Bumpy decided to be obedient for once, and swam to the wood. He stood on it, holding the rope with his teeth. The sailors pulled hard, and up came Bumpy and the piece of wood together.

Bumpy was delighted to see Tubby Bear and

Noddy. He rushed all round, shaking himself vigorously and sending hundreds of drops of water everywhere. The Captain heard all the noise and came out of his cabin to see what was going on.

"Wuff!" said Bumpy happily, and leapt at

him. Then he stood beside him, shaking himself again and wetting the Captain from head to foot.

"AVAST THERE, DOG!" roared the Captain, and Noddy and Tubby almost fell over in fright at such a loud voice. Bumpy was so scared that he rushed into the Captain's cabin and got under his bunk.

"WHAT'S ALL THIS?" said the Captain, glaring at Tubby and Noddy. "Stowaways? Ha—I'll show you what we do with stowaways!"

"Sir—this bear has joined us as a deck-hand," said a big sailor doll, saluting smartly. "The other fellow just leapt aboard—and we had to drag in his dog and tow his car behind."

"Ho—well, you'll have to sail with us now," said the Captain, looking at Noddy. "What's the matter with your head? Don't nod at me all the time!"

"No, Mr Captain, sir," said Noddy, his head nodding even faster in fright. "Oh, do please let me off the ship—and Tubby Bear too. He's run away to sea, sir, and . . ."

"Oh, he has, has he?" said the Captain. "Well, he'll soon wish he could run away back home. Dress him as a sailor, Mr Mate — and set him to work scrubbing the decks."

"Yes, sir!" said a sailor, saluting. He marched poor Tubby away. The Captain turned to Noddy.

"As for you, you're too small to do anything like that. You can be my cabin-boy—you'll have to clean my cabin well, and bring me my meals, and take my messages. And STOP NODDING YOUR HEAD AT ME!"

28

THE SAILOR SALUTED THE CAPTAIN AND THEN
MARCHED POOR TUBBY AWAY

29

"Yes, sir—I mean—no, sir," said Noddy, holding his head still with his hands. "Sir—about my car, I . . ."

"We'll tow it behind us," said the Captain. "It might come in useful when we land on Shell Island. You can drive me around then. Now—get somebody to find you some cabin-boy's clothes. AND BE QUICK ABOUT IT!"

"Yessir, yessir, yessir," said Noddy, trying not to nod his head. Good gracious—he was going to sea! Whatever would Big-Ears say if he knew!

"I shall be very homesick without my friends," thought Noddy, feeling that Tubby really couldn't be called a friend just now.

"WUFF!" said someone, and Noddy sat down very suddenly on the deck, while Bumpy-Dog licked him in delight.

"Well—at least I've got *you*," said Noddy, giving Bumpy a hug. "Stick close to me, Bumpy, please—I suddenly feel VERY lonely."

4. OUT AT SEA

A SAILOR took Noddy down into the ship, and gave him a cabin-boy's uniform. "I want to wear my hat with the bell," said Noddy. "This round cap-thing doesn't fit me. It will fall off every time I nod."

"All right. The Captain will certainly know where you are, every minute of the day, with that bell ringing all the time," said the sailor. "You seem a nice little fellow. Make sure you look after the Captain well, won't you?"

"Yes, I will," said Noddy. "I'm going to be as good a cabin-boy as I can. Where's that bear gone?"

"Here I am," said Tubby, and came up dressed like a sailor. Noddy stared at him.

"You look rather nice," he said. "I like your round hat. It suits you. Your mother and father sent me after you. You shouldn't have run away like that."

"I know," said Tubby. "I feel awfully homesick already."

"TUBBY! GET UP ON DECK!" yelled a voice. "THERE'S SCRUBBING TO DO!"

Tubby ran off at top speed. Noddy laughed. Tubby was going to work very hard on board ship!

"Now you go and tidy up the Captain's cabin," said the sailor. "You look a bit strange in those sailor's clothes. What about the dog? I've a good mind to dress him up in uniform too—it would make the Captain laugh!"

Bumpy ran away in alarm, and hid. Noddy went off to the cabin and tidied it up beautifully. He passed Tubby on the way back, he was scrubbing the deck and groaning.

"Oh my knees! Oh my back! Noddy, let's run away home!"

33

"*Swim* away, you mean!" said Noddy, crossly. "It's all because of *you* that I'm a cabin-boy, and Bumpy's here and my car's in the water, poor thing, being pulled along at top speed!"

The Captain was very pleased with Noddy's work that day. "You're a clever little fellow!" he said. "My cabin's all spick and span—and you're very quick at taking messages. How do you like life at sea?"

"Well—it's rather fun, sir," said Noddy. "And I do like the sailors, sir. They're always singing."

"I heard *you* singing too," said the Captain. "What song did you sing?"

"Oh, it was one I made up, sir," said Noddy. "It goes like this:

"I'm off on a trip
In a big, big ship,
Yo-ho for a life at sea!
The waves make a splash
And I make a dash
To take the Captain his tea!
The wind goes by,
And the waves are high,
And everything's wet as can be.
I'm kept on the run,
But really it's fun
For Tubby, Bumpy and me!"

"Ha!" said the Captain, smiling. "You sing that to the sailors tonight—it'll make them laugh!"

35

So Noddy sang his song that night, and everyone joined in heartily. Noddy nodded his head in time to the tune, and even Bumpy-Dog barked when the last line came with his name in it.

Noddy and Tubby were surprised to find they had no beds or bunks to sleep in. "Hammocks!" said Tubby, in alarm. "Hammocks for *beds!* I shall fall out of mine, I know I shall. I want to go home to my own nice little bed."

"Well, you shouldn't have run away," said Noddy, climbing into his hammock. "Oh no, Bumpy-Dog, I really can't have you in my hammock. *Please* get out!"

But Bumpy wouldn't. He settled himself in Noddy's hammock, and licked his toes without stopping. Noddy soon fell asleep, but Tubby cried for his mother. Oh, why had he run away? Why had he been so horrid, and silly and unkind?

In the night the wind blew hard, and the waves rose up high. The ship began to roll to and fro, to and fro, and Bumpy fell out of the hammock. BUMP!

He was very surprised and not at all pleased. He leapt in again, and Noddy groaned. "Oooh – *don't* leap on me like that. And STOP LICKING MY NOSE! Oh my goodness, that must have been a big wave, the ship went right on its side. Now Bumpy's fallen out again! Ha – he's jumped into the wrong hammock this time – my word, that sailor soon pushed him out!"

In the morning the waves were still very high. After Noddy had made sure that his little car was still being towed safely along behind the ship, he began to enjoy himself. He sang a little song, and all the sailors joined in.

"We're in for a storm,
We're in for a gale,
There might be a hurricane,
Blizzards and hail!
The sails are a-flap,
The waves are so high
That really and truly
They reach the sky!
Whoosh! goes the wind.
Flap! goes the sail.
But the ship's going bravely
Right through the gale!"

But somebody wasn't singing. Poor Tubby was feeling far too ill to sing. He was dreadfully seasick, and didn't want to do any work at all.

"What's the matter with you, moaning and groaning?" said a sailor, giving him a push. "Give a hand

38

POOR TUBBY WAS FEELING DREADFULLY SEASICK
AND FAR TOO ILL TO SING

with the sails, quick!"

"I want to go home," said Tubby. "I feel sick."

"Well, be sick all you like, but *go and give a hand with the sails!*" said the sailor. "What's the good of running away to sea if you want to go home? Why aren't you like that other fellow with the nodding head? He's cheerful enough. Now go and do what you're told!"

And poor Tubby had to stagger off to help with the flapping sails. Bumpy danced round him, trying to help. Then Tubby fell over, and nearly slid down the deck into the sea. Oh DEAR! Why ever did he run away?

5. THE LITTLE MERMAID

AFTER three or four days at sea Tubby felt
better – but how hard he had to work! Noddy
was really enjoying himself; and as for Bumpy, he
was having the time of his life.

The litle car still bobbed along, towed behind
the ship. Noddy often felt sorry for it. "Never
mind!" he called to it. "We're coming to an island
soon—then we'll take you ashore and you shall
have a run!"

But before they reached the island something
exciting happened. Noddy looked overboard—
and there was *someone in his car!* Yes, really! He
yelled to one of the sailors.

"Who's that in my car? It looks like a fairy doll
from the top of a Christmas tree."

"Well, it isn't—it's a little mermaid!" said the sailor. "My word—doesn't she look sweet in your car?"

"What's a mermaid?" said Noddy.

"Oh—mermaids live under the sea, and have tails instead of legs," said the sailor. "Isn't she having a wonderful time!"

The little mermaid was certainly enjoying herself! She waved to everyone, and pretended she was steering the car.

"The wind's gone right down," said Noddy. "I'm going to ask the Captain if I can dive into the sea and talk to that mermaid. The ship won't go, will it, now that there's no wind to blow it along?"

"No," said the sailor. "You ask the Captain, if you want. We might see a lot more of the little tailed creatures if you let them have rides in your car. I don't expect they've seen a car before!"

Off went Noddy to the Captain, who laughed loudly. "Mermaids! Well, well! So they've found your car, have they? Well, be careful *you* don't grow a tail too."

"I wouldn't like a tail," said Noddy. "I need my feet for the car pedals!" And away he went, back to the deck.

Splash! Noddy dived into the sea, and the little mermaid was so frightened that she disappeared under the water at once. Bumpy dived in too, but Tubby wouldn't. Noddy swam to his car and got into it. It was lovely to be sitting in his little car again, even if he couldn't drive it properly!

Soon a good many little heads appeared, bobbing about round the car. Mermaids— and mermen too! "I'll give you rides, if you like, while the ship isn't moving," called Noddy.

And now look at his car! You can hardly see it for mermaids and mermen. Noddy thought their tails were lovely.

When the wind began to blow a little, and the ship started to move slowly through the waves, the little fish-tailed folk cried out in delight, for then the car moved along too.

"Ahoy there!" called a sailor at last. "You're to come aboard, Noddy. Captain's orders. The wind's getting up and we're moving off. We're calling at Shell Island tomorrow."

Noddy said goodbye to the merfolk. One little mermaid swam deep down into the water and came up again with a pearl necklace. She hung it round Noddy's neck.

"Oh, thank you!" said Noddy. "If EVER I get home again, little Tessie Bear will love this necklace. I do like you mermaids and mermen. I hope you've enjoyed riding in my car!"

They waved goodbye as he climbed up a rope to the deck—and away went the lovely ship, her sails billowing once more, as the wind began to rise. The little car bobbed up and down behind, giving little parp-parps now and again, as if it wanted to tell everyone it was still there.

The pearl necklace was really pretty. Noddy wrapped it up and put it deep down in the pocket of his blue shorts, which were packed away in a drawer. How pleased Tessie would be!

On went the lovely ship—and on and on. Next day what a shout went up! "LAND AHOY! LAND AHOY!"

Everyone rushed to the side of the ship. "Shell Island!" said Noddy. "NOW my little car will be able to use its wheels again! LAND AHOY, little car!"

"PARP! PARP!" answered the car, happily. "PARP PARP!"

45

6. SHELL ISLAND

EVERYONE was very excited, and the Bumpy-Dog most of all. He tore round the decks, almost knocking over the Captain, and leapt up at Tubby and Noddy in joy. Down they went!

"I said '*Shell* Island', not '*Bone* Island', silly dog," said Noddy, getting up. "Now, if you knock me down again with one of those leaps of yours I won't take you on shore!"

It *was* fun to go ashore. The ship tied up at a little pier, and then everyone went on land, except for two sailors left on guard. Noddy's car was pulled up from the water and soon dried in the hot sun. "It will have to have some petrol," said Noddy. "Come here, Bumpy—let me tie you to the front of the car, and then you can pull it to the nearest garage."

So off went Bumpy-Dog, proudly pulling the

little car. It badly needed a clean, and was covered in bits of seaweed.

Shell Island was lovely. It seemed to be made of beautiful shells, of all colours and shapes and sizes. "I must take some home to your mother, Tubby," said Noddy.

"No," said Tubby at once. "*I'm* going to do that. I've missed her so dreadfully. I'm going to take the nicest shells I can find, so that she can make a border all round our flower-beds with them."

"What a good idea!" said Noddy. "I'll take some for Big-Ears—and yes, I might take some for Mr Plod as well. I've missed him quite a bit, though not so much as dear old Big-Ears!"

47

What a wonderful time they had on Shell Island! When the little car had been cleaned up, and filled with petrol, the Captain stepped in for a ride round the island. Noddy was very proud to drive him. He thought the Captain was marvellous!

"Sing me one of your songs," commanded the Captain as they drove off together, with Bumpy in the back, licking Noddy's ear every now and again. So Noddy sang.

"Here we go,
The Captain and I,
Riding on land
That is nice and dry!
The sea is wet,
And terribly salt,
Though I know of course
That it's not its fault.
The waves are enormous,
And when they break
You'd be surprised

48

NODDY WAS VERY PROUD TO DRIVE THE CAPTAIN
ROUND THE ISLAND

49

At the noise they make!
But here on the shore
It's steady and still,
No heaving about
To make you ill!
We're all in my car
As happy can be,
The Bumpy-Dog,
And Captain—and ME!"

"Very good," said the Captain. "You might ask the Bumpy-Dog not to breathe *quite* so hard down my neck. Now—let's go and get some shells. I know the best places for those!"

It was fun to go hunting for shells with the Captain because he really did know where

the finest ones were to be found. He and Noddy had brought a sack each, and they wandered about putting all kinds of lovely shells into their sacks. They left Bumpy in charge of the car because he kept getting under the Captain's feet.

50

"He's a very nice dog," said the Captain. "But I like him better when he's a long, long way away from me. Tell me, Noddy, who are you getting all these shells for?"

So Noddy told him all about Big-Ears and Tessie Bear and Mr Plod and the Wobbly Man. The Captain thought they sounded very nice. "I'd like to meet them one day," he said.

"Oh YES!" said Noddy, delighted. "I'm sure Big-Ears will give a party when we get back home. DO come, Captain. It would be a very great honour—especially as I am only your cabin-boy. Oh, I hope Big-Ears will like these shells. I might give Miss Fluffy Cat some too and Sally Skittle. I simply can't WAIT to get home now, Captain."

"Well, Tubby feels the same," said the Captain. "I don't think he'll run away again somehow, do you?"

Soon they were back on board the ship, and sailing off once more—home again this time, for the Captain had delivered all his sacks of goods at Shell Island, and was now homeward bound. Home! How lovely that word sounded!

"Home to my little House-For-One," thought Noddy. "Home to my little bed—and my lovely garden. Home to my own teapot, and my own chair. I'll see Big-Ears . . . I'll see . . . oh everyone. I'll even be glad to see Mr Plod!"

And now look, they're sailing away again, leaving Shell Island behind them. Noddy put his arm round Bumpy-Dog, and squeezed him hard. Then he lifted up one of Bumpy's ears and whispered into it.

"Home, Bumpy, HOME! What do you think of *that!*"

7. IT'S LOVELY TO BE HOME!

THE lovely ship sailed all the way back to the little stone jetty in Toyland. HOW excited Noddy and Tubby were!

"Look—we're almost there! Quick, Tubby, jump off with the others and make the ship fast with ropes. Oh, we're back again! Oh, I can't wait to go back to Toy Town and see everyone. Where's my car? Where's Bumpy? Oh, there you are!"

The car was safely on deck now, for the Captain had said it had better not be towed behind the ship any longer, and Noddy had spent a long time cleaning it. "Parp-parp!" it said, softly, knowing that it would soon be back in its own little garage.

"Noddy! Here is your pay," said the Captain,

putting a bag of money into Noddy's hands. "And I've paid Tubby too, though not so much as you. We'll be here for a week, so let me know when we can meet your friends."

"Oh, I will, I will!" said Noddy, who was now dressed in his usual clothes. He felt quite strange without the long trousers he had been used to wearing on board. "Come on, little car. Tubby, where are you? Bumpy, pull the car down off the deck for us."

"Goodbye!" cried the sailors, as Noddy, Tubby and Bumpy set off in the little car. "See you soon!"

"Goodbye!" called Noddy, feeling very happy indeed. A bag of money! A sack of shells! A pearl necklace! Goodness, he was rich, and he had presents for all his friends!

What excitement there was when Noddy drove through the streets he knew so well. Mr Plod couldn't say a word, he was so surprised. Noddy leapt out of his car and hugged him.

"Mr Plod! Dear Mr Plod! I'm back again. Oh, we've had such an adventure!"

"But where have you BEEN?" demanded Mr Plod. "You just disappeared in your car, and nobody heard any more about you. We have all been very sad and frightened. We were afraid you had gone for ever."

"I went to sea!" said Noddy. "I didn't mean to, though. I'll tell you all about it soon. Where's Big-Ears? Oh, Mr Plod, I'm so happy to be back again."

"And what about that naughty Tubby?" said Mr Plod, sternly. "Running away like that and making his mother so unhappy!"

55

"I'm very sorry about that," said Tubby, humbly. "I'm going to be good for ever now. Come on, Noddy—let's go home. I DO want to see my mother and father, and give them my shells."

So Noddy drove Bumpy and Tubby home—and oh, how very pleased and happy Mr and Mrs Tubby Bear were to see them! They all cried big

tears of happiness, and hugged one another like— well, just like bears! Noddy went into his own little house, and stared round in delight.

"My little House-For-One! You're nicer than I remembered. How tidy and clean you are—I wonder who's been scrubbing your floor? Why are you barking, Bumpy?"

"WUFF, WUFF, WUFF!" Bumpy rushed to the

front gate—and there was little Tessie Bear with Big-Ears! They had heard Noddy was back.

How they hugged him, and how his head nodded making his bell jingle loudly! "You're back! We were beginning to think you were gone for ever!" said Tessie, almost crying with joy.

Big-Ears clapped him on the back. "So you've been to sea—well, well, what will you do next! And you've brought back that rascal of a Tubby, I see! Welcome home, Noddy."

"I kept your house clean for you, Noddy," said Tessie, slipping her little paw into his hand. "I knew you'd come back."

"You *are* kind, Tessie Bear," said Noddy. "I've brought you a present. Look!" And he put his hand into his pocket and brought out a paper parcel. Tessie unwrapped it and gave a squeal of delight.

"OH! A pearl necklace! Oh, Noddy, NODDY! For me! Goodness, I never in my life thought anyone would give me such a lovely present. I'll put it on!"

Tessie looked sweet in it and Noddy was very pleased. Then he gave Big-Ears the sack of beautiful shells. "For your garden and mine," he said. "And some for Mr Plod too — to put round the edges of the flower-beds."

"Wonderful!" said Big-Ears, astonished. "Thank you, Noddy — you are a kind little fellow. My word, Mr Plod and I will enjoy ourselves making our gardens beautiful with these!"

"AND I've got a bag of money!" said Noddy. "And please, Big-Ears, I want to give a party with you — a sort of welcome-home one so that you can meet the Captain *and* all the sailors. They don't sail for a few days, so ..."

"A party! Yes, of course!" said Big-Ears. "And we'll ask EVERYONE! We'll have an open-air party, with tables down the street. What fun!"

"Wuff," said Bumpy in a small voice. He was feeling rather out of things. Tessie dropped upon one knee beside him.

"Darling Bumpy! I've missed you so. You shall come to the party too, and I'll buy you a lovely big blue bow."

The Tubby Bears were very pleased with Tubby's beautiful shells, too. It really was a joyful time. Even Mr Plod kept saying how nice it was to have Noddy and his car back again, though he wasn't so sure about the Bumpy-Dog!

Then came the day of the party! What a long, long table there was, all the way down the street, full of delicious food. And oh, flags and balloons were everywhere! Everyone sat down and listened to the Captain's speech, telling them what a fine cabin-boy Noddy was!

"Hurrah! Hurrah! Hurrah! Three cheers for Noddy! Two cheers for Tubby! One cheer for Bumpy! Hurrah! Hurrah for the Captain! Hurrah for everyone!"

What a noise! What excitement! Then Big-Ears banged on the table for silence. "Speech, Noddy, speech!" he cried. But Noddy shook his head.

"I can't make speeches!" he said. "But I've just thought of a new song. I'll sing it for you!"

And this is the song he sang:

> "We're home again, home again,
> Isn't it fun!
> We've been far away,
> But our journey is done.
> We've missed you all badly,
> Especially Big-Ears,
> And dear little Tessie,
> But now it's three cheers.
> We're all home again,
> Just as safe as can be,
> Mad little Bumpy-Dog,
> Tubby and me!"

And now just LISTEN to the clapping!

THE NODDY LIBRARY